W9-BSQ-115

STAR WARS
FORCES OF DESTINY™

MEET THE HEROES

WRITTEN BY ELLA PATRICK

ART BY GHOSTBOT & HASBRO

Disney • LUCASFILM PRESS

Los Angeles • New York

Printed in the United States of America

First Edition, August 2017

1 3 5 7 9 10 8 6 4 2

Library of Congress Control Number on file

FAC-029261-17174

ISBN 978-1-368-01121-1

A long time ago in a
galaxy far, far away,
many girls were fighting
for what was right.

They came from different planets.
They lived during different times.
But each girl was strong
in her own way.
And they were all destined to be heroes.

Here are just a few. . . .

Meet Rey.

Rey is a scavenger and a pilot.

Rey is brave.

Rey lives on the desert planet of Jakku.

Her home is an old AT-AT.

Rey zooms across the desert
on her speeder.
She searches crashed ships for parts.

Then she sells the parts to
the mean alien Unkar Plutt.

Rey rescued BB-8 when he
was lost in the desert.

Meet Leia.

Leia is a princess and a general.

Leia is smart.

Leia relies on two droids for help.

R2-D2 is an astromech droid.
He is short and silver.

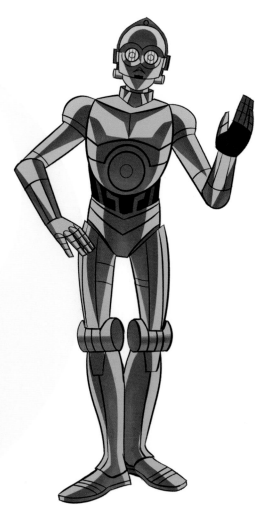

C-3PO is a protocol droid.
He is tall and gold.

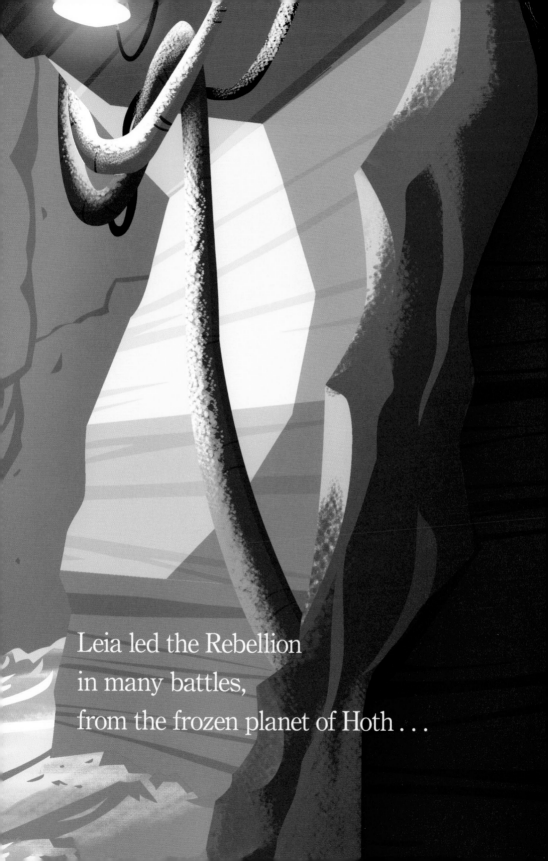

Leia led the Rebellion
in many battles,
from the frozen planet of Hoth . . .

. . . to the forests of Endor.

Meet Jyn.

Jyn is a soldier and a spy.

Jyn is tough.

Jyn is not afraid to face danger
for a worthy cause.

Meet Sabine.

Sabine is a rebel and an artist.

Sabine is creative.

Sabine and her droid friend Chopper
like to make trouble for the Empire.

You can tell from Sabine's helmet
that she is from the planet Mandalore.

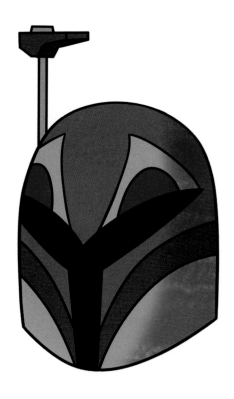

Mandalore is known for its
strong warriors.

But Sabine is also artistic.
She likes to add color to her world.

Meet Hera.

Hera is a captain and a leader.

Hera is loyal.

Hera flies a fast ship.

Hera's ship is called the *Ghost.*

Meet Ahsoka.

Ahsoka is a Jedi and a warrior.

Ahsoka is strong.

Ahsoka had many teachers.
Yoda was a very old and wise Jedi.

Anakin Skywalker was a
young and powerful Jedi.

Ahsoka has two lightsabers to protect the people she cares about.

Meet Padmé.

Padmé is a queen and a senator.

Padmé is kind.

Padmé lives on the
busy planet of Coruscant.
She works in the Senate
with other leaders to make
the galaxy a better place.

These girls are just some of the brave heroes from a galaxy far, far away. You can be a hero, too!